TIME AND TIME AGAIN

TIME AND TIME AGAIN

Henry O'Hagan

iUniverse, Inc.
Bloomington

Time and Time Again

iUniverse books may be ordered through booksellers or by contacting:

iUniverse
1663 Liberty Drive
Bloomington, IN 47403
www.iuniverse.com
1-800-Authors (1-800-288-4677)

ISBN: 978-1-4620-2401-8 (sc)
ISBN: 978-1-4620-2402-5 (e)

Library of Congress Control Number: 2011912162

Printed in the United States of America

iUniverse rev. date: 07/27/2011

"You are on, get up, you are on, now!" A voice kept whispering in my ear.

"What! What! Oh –oh: We are alerted." I answered in a sleepy tone.

"Come on get up, briefing is at 0430 and its 0400; the officers were up over an hour ago. And be quite the others are still sleeping." The voice was insistent.

"OK, I am awake but why today? We were altered yesterday, weren't we? No that was the day before, time seems to stand still." I answered not knowing if the voice was listening. "OK wake up the rest of the guys."

I started dressing. Get the long johns on I told myself. We are probably flying at 28000. I bumped into guys going and coming from the latrine. No words spoken as the voice said the others, meaning the other 2 crews were still asleep, no need to wake them. We left the Quonset hut for the briefing room which was just a larger version of the one we left. As we entered the blackout doorway there was coffee and toast with marmalade on a table. I thought this time it must be a long mission as the cooks were up early and the CO did not like food at briefings, don't kick about the food just enjoy a quick bite, even though I hate marmalade.

As I was sipping my coffee I spotted our Captain sitting in the 2nd row. This meant that we would be flying wing to the leader and if anything happened to the 1st plane then we took over. I nodded to the Captain and waited for the rest to go in. Seating in the briefing has a protocol. Officers sit on the left and EM sit on the right. 4 chairs on the left 6 chairs on the right in order left, Pilot, Copilot, Navigator, Bombardier, to the right engineer, radio operator (that's me), armor gunner, nose gunner, top turret gunner, and lastly tail gunner.

We no sooner got seated when in a loud voice the command 'Attention' was issued everyone stood erectly. The Colonel strode in to the room and straight to the platform.

"At ease, but no smoking: Gentlemen we have an important target today, it is a long way there and a long way back. We are going to bomb a munitions factory, reputedly a very productive one, so be sharp and drop your bombs where they will hit the buildings and not the cows in the fields." The CO was meaning what he said. "Next I will be in the lead plane as an observer. The pilot, Captain Shays, will be the ships commander. Major Browne, our air exec will detail the flying arrival positions and times. Now I want you to know we will be flying at 25000 to 28000 this will be top squadron max height, so beware of the ME109's and FW190's coming out of the sun. Flack will be heavy around the factory so no fighters to contend, they will reappear when we are on our return. Good luck and good bombing." The CO ended with a slight smile.

There was some murmuring and no one spoke up, Major Browne took the floor."Get your coffee refills and toast while I set up the camera." This took ten minutes then he started with fuel loads, ammo capacity, and bomb type and how many in each plane. Then he said, "Take off will be difficult with the load and the need to conserve fuel, you will need almost 90% of the runway." This last statement brought a gasp from every one. "This can be done but the airplane captain must pay strict attention to every detail," He added.

The rest was technical stuff and Navigators were given the routes to and from target area, Bombardiers the altitude for max bomb coverage and RO's the frequencies to monitor, a special freq is always given that would be the recall number. That was briefing except the last by the CO.

"You have 45 minutes for mess, and to preflight. Don't dawdle. And be sure you are not late at rendezvous or I will have a few choice words with the late comers when we return," The CO said as he marched from the room.

Mess was nothing to write home about. But on mission days there were real eggs and real milk and some bacon plenty of coffee. The only trouble no one ate much. We talked mostly about home and family and the army, then griped about everything.

"My girlfriend writes that I must be enjoying the flying all over Europe. In the last letter she wanted to know if I had been able to get to Paris! Can you believe this? She doesn't have a clue what is happening and what I do. She thinks we have a quite life just enjoying the sights. I don't tell her anything in my letters. You know what I mean." Enos the ball gunner telling about his girl back home.

"Yeah, I met this broad; she was a cheerleader at the rival High School. I was a cheerleader at my school and we met at a rally. Boy was she good looking. I didn't think I had a chance to date her I mean I am short that's why I was a cheerleader instead of a jock. At the end of the rally we were all together and I asked if she like to go to the dance that Saturday and she said yes. We had a great time and as I was taking her home she said why we didn't go to lovers' lane. I think I put the petal down almost through the floor board, and there we were hopping into the back seat. No conversation just started necking. Then as I tried to get serious she slapped my hand. All we did was heavy petting. Man I can't wait to go back home and look her up." Ben sighed as he thought about his love life.

"You are nuts she probably met a defense worker and is married." Added Andy the nose turret gunner.

"Maybe she went to college and met a wealthy 4fer and now has lots of kids," Scoffed Enos the ball turret gunner.

"I thought flying was going to be fun plus the pay was the best but these long missions take all the joy out of the whole war." Mick the engineer groused. "Maybe the next one will be a milk run."

"I sure miss my Mom's biscuits and gravy for breakfast; maybe, if I asked she could send the cooks the recipe." Andy the nose gunner said amid many oh yea's from the rest of the guys..

Then we filed out into the waiting trucks and rode to our B-24.

We gathered under the Starboard wing and our captain said get busy preflight if anything looked iffy tell him right away. That was it no speeches no send offs just do your job and do it right.

The Pilot and I had our work cut out as we had to sync the radios so he could press a button and listen to any and all radio sets. Since there were 4 sets and 4 freq.'s on three sets to monitor I made sure he knew which button to press and with radio silence it was essential that he could not make a mistake. I took away all other crew members stations by the simple twist of the knob that enabled one to hear and send. I left the intercom intact.

I went to the meeting of the GOD squad on the tarmac. Word must have gotten around that this was a big mission. Usually one of the guys led a short prayer, but today a priest, a rabbi and a minister all attended, each gave a quick word and then we all scrambled to our aircraft. Take off was eminent.

Take off in a bomber is always exciting; a loaded B24 has 1800 gallons of high octane fuel, top that off with a ton or more of unarmed high explosives, plus 10 men with guns and ammo, one begins to wonder if an overloaded plane can actually fly. Our airplane made it off the ground and we did not need 90% of the run way. The takeoff was at 0547 military time, ten hours to and from the target meant we should touchdown at about 1600 hours.

At this point all I did was monitoring the frequencies which were blank, no air traffic to give away our position to the enemy, still we had to make sure there was no recall from bomber command. Our pilot, Capt. Richards, had the heading so we started to climb. At 13000 he gave the command to put on the oxygen masks this meant about 9 hours of an uncomfortable leather and rubber contraception on all our faces. We hit rendezvous right on the button and headed right out to the target, of course evasive action and change of headings was necessary.

Mick and the Bombardier brought the coffee around offering the sandwiches of which none were eaten. After we hit the coast line a few fighters could be seen a long way off, they were determining our speed altitude and heading. It wasn't long before the real fighters arrived and the fun began. These enemy pilots knew all the tricks, come at us from the sun, dive from above spraying bullets, climb up from below, or head in from 12 o'clock while doing a roll. I usually manned a waist gun but since we were number 2 Mick had to take that job and I maintained the radios. Not one of our planes took a critical hit. Some minor damage and later we found that one of the gunners on the lead plane got the million dollar wound meaning he got shot in the butt.

Conversation was and always is scarce on a B24. You can hardly talk with an oxygen mask over your nose and mouth then there is the noise factor, no one ever told us about decibels. Then add bone chilling cold, at times the thermometer reads 60% below zero, try moving around while dressed in wool wrapped in some kind of animal skin it's almost impossible to turn your head. This uniform runs from your feet the boots are made from the same material as the pants and jacket all topped off with a cap with a face mask to breathe oxygen. I would bet a month pay that most could not walk a city block. On the intercom the Capt limits the talk to only spotting the incoming craft and ACK-ACK. A throat microphone really doesn't allow conversation just a few words. No one has time to carry on small talk.

The fighters left us. I suppose they went after bigger game. Our squadron kept a tight formation this is crucial to fend off the attacking planes. With 10 .50 caliber machine guns pointing at you and bullets flying around it doesn't take a genius to figure that one just might hit a important part of the engine like fuel lines. These fighters understood about tight formations.

Pretty soon the antiairflack began, this meant the auto pilot would change headings and altitude to confuse the gunners. One shell came close,about 50 yards on the port side, we all heard the metal hit the fuselage. Sometimes ACK-ACK can be more freighting than a direct attack by a ME109. A fighter starts at the head on (12O'clock) continues around to the tail (6O'clock), Port side is 9O'clock this makes starboard side 3O'clock. If you are on the intercom you know exactly where the enemy is attacking. With ACK-ACK the shell isn't visible until the explosion takes place then a big black cloud of deadly shrapnel is plainly in sight, unless the shell fires inside the ship or close by, all you feel is the explosion.

The target was visible and Joe our Bombardier went to the front and started his routine as soon as the IP came into his viewer he took over control of the airplane put the target in the cross hairs and bombs away. Losing a ton of weight the airplane rose a few feet and the speed increased.

The pilot did a 180 turn to starboard, reassembled and started for home. My most important job was to radio the strike report. This time it was encoded. I had written down the codes in the order, very good, good, just missed, no hits. I had written these on rice paper. The target was hit right in the middle, the message I sent was very good as soon as I could make out where the bombs hit. I consumed all but the original rice paper, which I kept for the Pilot to enter in the log book. Our Bombardier was always accurate and I could see the hits from my window.

For some reason the enemy did not come after us but the

antiairflack did take out one of the groups' planes. 10 men died in a flash of a direct hit. No one on our craft saw the actual hit and explosion; just as well as we all were buddies with our counterpart on that crew.

Then the flack just stopped but we knew some where the enemy gunners were tracing our every move so to be on the lookout was our number 1 job at this point

"Crew this is the pilot." His voice came over the intercom; at first his voice had a startling effect. "I want everyone to be on special alert. This is when if we relax bad things happen. Also I want every station to report, now. Start with the Nose, then Upper turret, follow with the Ball then Starboard, then Port and last Tail. Tell what you see and sign off. Out:"

"Roger, nose, all clear no planes no antiaircraft, out:"

"Roger, top, I see a plane or two in the long distance can't make out type. Out:"

The reports kept up until all had reported. Looks like the 109's went hunting elsewhere.

"Pilot to RO: RO come to the front deck and bring your light. Out:" Capt's voice sounded urgent.

Everything you would use was in its place in the small space called the radio station, I grabbed the signal lamp went on deck.

"I am here," shouting in the pilot's ear so he could hear above the noise and the headset.

"See what the lead is asking by code on the lamp. I will scoot over so the Co. Pilot can take the controls. Ok Co, take over." This was with the Capt listening and speaking while wiggling to vacate his seat.

I was able to see the window of the lead plane and in essence their Capt and the CO wanted us to take the over the lead, it was because one of the bullets had gotten a junction box and the radio was dead. The CO and Pilot had received scratches from a shell exploding near the bomb bay while open. Also was news that the Tail gunner was hurt, no details. Changeover would occur in 2 minutes after the lead plane moved forward of the formation.

The change took place without incident. This maneuver is tricky because behind your plane are up to 19 aircraft trying to stay close. The lead pulls forward about 500 feet then slowly moves right and down, while your ship speeds up and moves left the other ship slows and lets the other ships catch up in the meantime your pilot slows the aircraft and lets the whole formation catch into the new 'V' shape.

"RO I want to signal the other planes what has happened and it must be in today's code. I want to do this on the UHF radio, OK. Out:" Capt's voice came over the intercom and I was already complying as I anticipated this move.

"Capt, this is the code words you will use on channel 3. RED DOG S. NOW DOG 2 IN FRONT, PUPPY OK. Out:" I use the code of the day and hour. Very short so their radar or radio operators could not get a fix. I also return to the cockpit and use the light to signal the CO.

"RO, is there anyone else that can monitor the radios? I want you to have a break as after we clear the coast I will need you and the navigator to work together. Out:" The Capt had spoken.

"Pilot, yes the Port gunner can monitor but can't send messages. Out:" I answered.

When we left the enemy's coast the pilot started the descent and it wasn't long before the oxygen masks came off and the balance of the coffee now just tepid, was drank without a complaint plus we ate the cardboard chicken sandwich, at least this was what was listed on the package. There was some talk between those that could walk around, it was more like yelling at each other.

Just as I was settling in, Joe Kielly bombardier had followed me to the waist. "Want me to take over? I have no duties now that the bombs have been jettisoned. The nose compartment is crowded I need some room to breathe." Yelling was the only way we could communicate without the intercom.

"Sure thing I could use the time as I have been listening to nothing on the blank frequencies. Occasionally I hear a voice of a plane in trouble or lost. Otherwise silence," I answered yelling.

I sat on the deck just behind the Ball turret and pulled out a note book of rice paper. The CO would have a fit and I would be court marshaled if anyone knew what I was doing. I kept notes only up to date on the current mission; all others were in my foot locker back at base, so no one if captured could learn much more than they already knew. I jotted down the date and the mission and the number our crew, had flown hard to believe but this was number 14 only 11 more to go after this one. The crew had changed since the 1st sortie, so I listed each name to make sure I would not forget who was with me. Pilot Richard Richards, Co pilot James Thomason, Navigator Wes Wills, Bombardier Joe Kielly, Engineer Mick Raymound, Nose Gunner Andy Wynne, Top Turret Gunner Jim Knottes, Waist Gunner Chet Murray, Ball Gunner Enos Beckker, Tail Gunner Ben Turner, lastly Radio Operator Erick Horseman. I sorted of dozed off then a kick from Joe woke me up, the Capt wanted me. I made one stop at the bulkhead just before the Bomb bay as this is where the relief tube is located, After 9 hours of flying I needed that.

"RO to Pilot: Yes, Capt I am here at my station. Out:" I used the intercom to answer.

"Pilot to All: Good. Everybody listen only Erick, Wes and I will use the phone as we are now over our home route and we need direction with so much evasive flying we aren't sure just where we are located. Wes, give us a heading. Out:"

"Navigator to Pilot: Start at 15 degrees and I will correct unless Erick has a more precise head. Out:" He spoke in short bursts.

"RO to Pilot; Radio compass is right on except that we can refine that to 17 degrees. Out:" I answered.

Since we had taken the lead the rest of the group, 20 planes, were following us to base. Wes and I made a couple of corrections so we could do a flyover the field, a tradition since WWI. We got the signal flare and the Port Wingman started the chandel which is a 180 climbing turn, after the turn with wheels and flaps down we slowly descend, touchdown and then taxi to hardstand. End of flight.

I can tell you that seeing the airfield coming into view was like coming home. It is relief yet you feel exhausted.

After landing you take time to police the space, 1st the ground crew appreciates the neatness and if you don't these guys will let you know. 2nd you have to occupy the same area sometime the next few days. Some of the men start talking like 100 miles per hour, the sentences are sort of just gibberish no vowels and a lot of profanity. The Captain was different.

"Men I would like thank you for a job well done. Every one performed in a business way. See you at debriefing." The skipper said these words as he jumped into the jeep and headed to the hut.

I know that other crews were shall we say more cordial,

lot of first name and kidding between the officers and EM but our Captain was an airline pilot before the war and he like to keep everything GI according to the book. He was addressed as Captain Richards except on the intercom then it was Pilot. The Co Pilot was Lt. Thomason, the Navigator was LT. Wills, and the Bombardier was Lt. Kielly and again on the inter it was their station not name.

The trucks were waiting and we climbed into the back. It was understood that we did not discuss the mission before debrief so the ride was short and quiet except for Mick who carried on a monologue about farm life and how he did not mind us getting up at 0400 as he always had to milk the cows that early each morning. Talk about BS Mick could sling it, all day every day.

We entered the hut where we left early that morning, only it didn't seem that it was the same day. The room was quite pandemonium guys were talking to the debrief officers others were standing around drinking coffee, water and the usual shot of whiskey. I don't know how this practice started but it was traditional for those that wanted a quick pick up, some did not take the libation still others would ask to have more, this request was always refused. It seemed ages since we walked in but finally we were seated and our friend at the morning Brief was our debrief officer. He didn't ask each what they saw but just said to everybody what did you see. The Captain went first and told about the encounter with the fighters then the flack and the bomb run. Nothing that was seen was viewed as spectacular, just the facts over and over, nothing was recorded unless we all had heard and seen for ourselves, in other words no guessing.

Suddenly the whole room became very quite. The tail gunner from the last squadron was reporting.

"I was scanning the skies using both my eyes and the gun sight." Tail gun charley was reciting the details. "Captain Early's plane was very visible since he had left his position in the flight pattern, I thought he was having problem with one of the engines, he was trying to catch up, but was flying in a straight line no evasive action, and all of a sudden a flash and the whole ship was engulfed in flames. I know what you all wonder and no there were no chutes."

"Did you notice which engine was giving Early's plane trouble?" Major Browne was doing his duty to find the cause.

"It seemed to be number three, it was out of snyc, they were close to us about 100 yards when they got hit" The tail gunner could not answer any more. Debriefing broke up.

CHAPTER 2

THE CREW BROKE INTO GROUPS our EM's gather around Mick and me.

"Does anyone want to eat, the mess hall is open and the cooks always go all out for the meal?" I asked to no one in particular.

"Why not, the last time I ate anything was last night and besides the only other thing to do is shower, shave and hit the sack." Mick was at his usual best, giving advice but not really advising.

"I'm tired but still excited and will be until I shower so let's eat." I answered.

Five of us went to the mess hall. Chet the younger of the crew and had only joined us after we lost a gunner on mission 9, said see you later then left for the Quonset.

"He did not sleep much last night." Jim who paled around with Chet offered. "It seems that his family had tried to discourage the desire to join the Air Corps. So when he was assigned to us and found that he was replacing a gunner that had been shot he became very worried." Jim added.

"Go after him and make sure that he joins us for chow. And don't take no for an answer." I spoke with conviction. "Jim, make sure he knows he is wanted and he is welcome but that this is a must that all stick together. I figured that he might be a loner but that as a crew we do certain things together. Get going." Jim raced as I spoke.

At mess the cooks had prepared lots of different types of food so you had a choice from a full meal to just sandwiches and even some eggs (dried of course). Lots of coffee, can milk or powdered milk, and what passed to be cookies. Jim and Chet joined us and all made room for them. Some kidding always ensues.

"Jim, what did you do in School, track, Last time I saw you move that quickly was when you were chasing a broad in London." Andy joined in the ribbing.

"I could beat every one of this group in a foot race. I might even tie my shoelaces together. Or give you 9 yards head start in a 100 yard dash. And still beat you by a yard." Jim got right into the spirit.

We could see Chet start to take to this kind of comrade kidding, even though he did not actually say anything.

The mod quickly changed from morass to a comradre, a feeling of togetherness and being wanted. I yelled last one in the sack is a dirty dog, and ran toward the hut we call home. I opened the door and got a surprise.

"What are you guys doing here? I thought you would be in town or at the NCO club." I asked in a bewilder tone.

The other crews sort of answered in unison. You don't know? Everyone is alerted for tomorrow.

"The call is for 0530 so this means a local bomb run like the pens or wharfs. May be it will rain or the CO will have passes for everyone." Maguire said.

"That will be the day." A voice cried out. "Better still the enemy has given up and we are going home." The voice or maybe another added.

"Oh no not again I can't believe what you are saying." I was almost shouting.

"You better believe it. The notice is on the Bulletin Board. So it is not a joke. Maybe you should go read it for yourselves." Again it was the voice, and he was not laughing.

As this was taking place our crew as one was stripping for a shower but first a shave. You wanted to give your face a long rest before the oxygen mask had to go on. I then took a long shower and fell into the bunk. I was asleep as my head hit the pillow. It was 1900 hours.

I slept until sometime during the night when I did the nature call so had a chance to rationalize. If we had many more of these double duty raids then just maybe we will finish the 25 by the first of the year and home would be in the future not a dream but a reality. Back to the sack and this time dreaming, guess what.

THE DOOR BANGED AGAINST THE tin wall and a voice shouted: "Alright rise and shine! Briefing in 30 minutes and the EM will have a special brief in the mess. Is everybody happy?" The sergeant's voice seemed almost giddy.

Everybody in the hut, all 18 of the three crews were awake and grumbling, not like yesterday when the others were asleep. Lot of vulgarity and swearing. Why our group haven't we done enough of our share? This was the theme of the gripping.

Everybody but one straggler were on time and coffee cups were filled and we sat in groups of 6 all huddled together. Enter the EXCO Lt Col. Maxwell.

The order "Attention" was given by the Sgt. Major. This must be important ran through my head "At ease" again the Sergeant .Major ordered and everyone sat down.

"It's the pens again." Lt. Col. Maxwell spoke. "If you have forgotten that means the submarine base where repairs are made and new equipment is installed.

CHAPTER 3

This time it will be different, there will be 4 more groups so the armada will have between 105 max to 100 min. There will be 4 bombing runs, A high altitude, 2 side at minimum height, and 2 groups coming in low about 500 feet. Purdy will lead high and O'Conner and Bardot at the left and right. Richards will lead the two groups at low level. For the Richards crew your Pilot has been promoted he is a Major. Now that means Shays plane will be the wingman. For just a minute let's talk about the bombs, the high group will have high explosive contact types, the other two flights will have incendiaries', the lower will have a new type deep penetration. These are supposed to stop the use of the pens at least for a while. Strike report will be in code and should contain what you saw hitting the target, you should not see any results of the penetration bombs. Take off will be staggered so you will be at your plane at 0700. There will be escort service by spitfires and P51's this should keep the 109's away from your bombing group but beware the antiaircraft is accurate and there are plenty of guns protecting this site. Mess is now open."

We sat very still and quiet until Mick broke the spell.

"Let's eat, this is going to be a milk run, at least I hope so. Anyway we need to take care of the inner man." Mick uttered these while getting up grabbing a tray. He proceeded to load up on all the eggs and toast.

"Milk run, there is no such animal? You must be thinking of your farm. With 190's and 109's aiming at your ass." This was from Ben.

"And don't forget the 'AA' guns, every one of the gunners believes he's an Annie Oakley." This wisdom came from Andy.

Preflight was the same old same old, the only difference

was we all lined up and saluted our new Major and each shook his hand. Everything else was the same.

The takeoff was a lot better than yesterday shorter runway and lighter load as we did not need the extra gas. This run would be 5 hours top maybe shorter if the other formations kept to the plan and complied to take off and assembly formula. We assembled and lost about 15 minutes due to a late arrival of tail end charley, we were on our way. It was not too long when I started to hear some disturbing sounds on the radio. The most often was 'am hit' or 'we can't make the return', these words meant that the run into the target was being defended, after all the U-Boat was the first line of offense. Since my job was to be a gunner in the waist and Mick would take over the chores of the platform I just listened.

We were 15 minutes out from the pens when the first fighters found us. The 109's came in from 12 o'clock guns blazing and going side to side up and down right on top of these were our P-51's. Individual fights broke out all around us and like a passing parade the scene faded.

"Here comes two at 9o'clock low."

"Another at 12o'clock high with all guns firing."

"Watch out for the tail, one coming in from below. There's a high one at 6oclock even." The niceties were left out, no screaming just the facts, so beware.

I was manning the port gun. What did I think about when the enemy planes attacked? I always had fear unadulterated fear. Am I going to get it today? ('It' is being killed). Or worse yet a wound that will cripple me for life, losing a leg or arm. Then when you see the guns firing from the attacking plane you can hardly breathe. You know that you would like to hide but there is no place to hide, no fox holes in the sky, all of a sudden you are angry and start to fire your .50 Caliber as you were taught short bursts and be aware of the planes around you don't shot them down. I heard myself describing the flight of the enemy fighters. Suddenly the fighter broke off and you are left with a feeling of relief. Only realizing the ground guns would commence and more terror as the shells would be bursting very close.

"RO to Pilot: The fighters have broken off. Out:" I immediately went to the proper protocol of intercom calling.

The ACK-ACK came on heavy and pretty accurate we took a near miss on engine 4 which started running rough until the Pilot feathered the prop. The 'bombs away' was given by the Bombardier, we chandel to the port and started home.

The fighters reappear and were present for the next 20 or 30 minutes, some of the bullets came through the fuselage and this was scary, these shells ricochet you hear the first, then hear it two or three times before it is spent. So for the last half hour we were the targets. This wasn't the first time or the last time.

We headed home, as we flew over the North Sea the engine began to smoke black the consensus is an oil line has been ruptured, this is bad news. If a fire erupts in the engine cowling then we must bail out or worse ditch in the cold rough water.

"Pilot to crew: I think we will make landfall, so prepare to bail, the signal will be two short rings on the emergency bell when you hear this jump do not wait. I will be the last and direct the plane with auto pilot on to the North Sea. Then I will bail so I won't see you until we all get back to base, best of luck. Out:"

We made land fall and as soon as we were over level ground the bell rang two short bursts, everyone jumped I went out the back of the bomb bay as did the ball gunner while the waist and tail went out the escape hatch in the rear. I counted ten and pulled the release handle on the chute and the silk blossomed above me and I floated to the ground. Watching our ship smoking then fire broke out, hope the Pilot bailed I thought to myself. Gathering up the chute I could watch some of the others come down we were all close except the Major, we could barely see his chute. We didn't have to wait long when a jeep came in sight to rescue us and drive us back to the closest military hospital; really it was an aide station. We all had bumps and bruises not too serious I had twisted my ankle, the rest had landed on their butts so they had sore spots, scrapes mostly, The medics said we were ok and a truck drove us back to base, without pilot and plane.

1st stop was the base hospital. We all told the medic that aide station said we were fit and did not need any further treatment.

"Yeah, yeah," said the doctor, "But the manual says I have to look you over if and when you survive a parachute jump. So don't give me any lip just do as I say, now undress down to your skivvies. Oh by the way your pilot is resting in the officer's ward, he came in right from the landing, some burns but he will be ok."

After the medical exam we all were confined to the hospital for 3 days, either that or go to flack haven for a week. Every one chose the 3 days, this way we could stay as one crew and not have to fly any missions for at least 4 days. T.G.

CHAPTER 4

NEXT MORNING THE CREW ASSEMBLED informally in the sun room and rehashed the jump.

"I' m sure I hit that ME109 that was coming in head on." Andy the nose gunner was hoping for a kill, he needed confirmation so he was trying to enlist the minds of all of us for the needed help.

"I saw a lot of smoke when he dived away from us but I could not watch as I was busy with the shooting at the rear attackers." Ben the tail gunner affirmed the plane had been hit.

"Well have to wait for confirmation form the following group, so let's not worry about that one hit." Our pilot spoke.

The Major had given debrief to the CO, so no need for the rest to add what was now old news. Each left the room singly and I hung around to talk to the Major.

"RO you want something?" The Major sensed that I wanted to talk.

"Right to the point, I want to interview all the

crew and I would need your permission and your help with the Officers. This is for posterity as we as individuals and a group it might mean something as we grow older. I want to promise I am not going to publish this missal until the war is over for a long time and it may be that it will never see the light of day. I am not sharing this with anyone and just in case something should go wrong I will place this in a special envelope to be sent home to my father and then he will decide to keep or destroy." I spoke in a confidential voice.

"You have a right smart idea. All groups have a historian; the individual is just a footnote. If your writing just for the crew then I say let's do it right. What will you need, pen pencil paper? I will give the Ok to the officers and you tell the EM it's OK with me. Any one balk, come see me." The Major added, "When do you want to start?"

"Today and you are first." I smiled when I said that. "Oh if you could find a typewriter that's not in use it would save an editors eyesight, some day."

Right after noon mess the Major called to me and said. "I have a small room that is not being used shall we start"

"This is a great time, the rest are getting in extra sack time so I have paper and pencils let's begin." I spoke with some excitement in my voice.

The room was very small a chair for each of us and the table was really a hospital tray. I started the interview by asking a few basic questions, then sat back and wrote as quickly as I knew how using a type of shorthand.

CHAPTER 5

THE MAJORS RESPONSE:

"I was born on August 1 1909 in a city in the Midwest. I grew up in a very normal way. My father was working in a metal shop and when airplanes became a rage he rose from foreman to supervisor. After school I would go down to meet him. That was when I started to clean up the floors, sometimes the boss would pay me, especially if business was good. The shop became an airplane machine shop fabricating parts and on the side building engines. This is when I became interested in flying. One afternoon, I worked later than my father, an older man whom I had seen around asked if I would like to ride in a plane. The next Saturday I went to the field where there were some aircraft and there was this man. He took me for a ride and to tell the truth I still get thrilled as I did that day. I went to college got a degree but I still wanted to fly. There weren't any schools to teach flying so one had to learn on his own. I hung around the field where the only real business was crop dusting. Flyers used the old flying Jenny of WWI fame. There were some two seaters were availablean one could fly for a fee, I would help with the dusting the only pay was lessons from the flyers.

Our town was growing and soon there was a small airline that had two old Ford Trimotors and started some routes. At first I would ride and although I was not listed as a co-pilot that was my main job. When the draft started I was exempt but one of the employees of the airline told me if I really wanted to learn to fly then join the Army Air Corps. I did just that and well here I am a Major flying the biggest and best airplanes in the world. I am married to one of the sectaries and we have two small children. This sort of brings my life to date."

"What does flying in combat mean to you? Do you think of home or the fact that this is very dangerous?" I asked this question in varying degrees to all the members of the crew.

"Oh I know that this can be very stressful so I think mostly of the family, which brings me to a reality that I may stay in the service once this ugly business is finished. Air line flying is boring and then the flights can take lots of time. At route end you may be asked to fly to another city and home maybe weeks away. If I can obtain a staff position then I will keep on serving, maybe as an instructor or later an administrator. This is of course conjecture, now to get the job done

————

The co-pilots response;

"I was born in 1919 and my childhood was not as ideal you would think. So let's skip that, and go on to high school. I was a 3 sport letterman: football, basketball, baseball. I got a scholarship to one of the southern universities to play football and baseball, the latter held some promise for me and I was scouted by the major leagues, but here comes the war I'm drafted and lucked out, I become a cadet in the Army Air Corps. I was blessed with athletic ability so flying school was not difficult. I passed and became a 2nd Lt. Army Brass said I was a likely candidate for 4 engines training, as you know no choice was given so here I am. I can hardly wait for this to be over so I can pursue my baseball career. Oh I am single and no girl friends to write or receive mail."

"How does serving in the military in a war affect you?" I asked a leading question.

"Freighting, always scared, some nights are sleepless. But mainly sitting next to the Major and most of the time I just sit. When the bullets and flack start I am angry, I have nothing to fight back with, I am thinking this is going to be my last or sometime I hope that the pilot stays healthy and I don't have to take the awesome responsibility of flying this ship at this time. I am going to survive and live out my dream. Oh I haven't told anyone about my dream I am playing ball it is the bottom of the 9th and the bases are loaded I take a two ball count then hit a home run. I wake up. I am going to do this someday and I hope it is in the big leagues."

Navigator response:

"I was born 1920 in Berkeley California not far from the University. My childhood was normal although I preferred the library to playing games. I graduated from high school with very good grades and since the U was so close I could study and still hold small jobs locally. I graduated again with good grades. I was an electrical engineer so when I enlisted in the A.A.C. It was logical to study Navigation, I am not being boastful but the whole class was easy and I passed with honors and became a 2nd Lt. I am afraid I am not a colorful person and my story will never make for a full novel. Answering the last question, I am engaged and we write regularly."

"How does flying in combat compare with your ideas of serving your country?" I enquired.

"That is a question I ask myself every day. My answer is that I think only about survival, I want this crazy war to end then I can go home. Someday I want to be an engineer and build a building at least five stories high."

———

Bombardier response:

"Erick, why do you want to interview me? I am just an ordinary guy. Oh sure my father was very wealthy, in fact he owned just about everything in town. I had a roadster when I went to High School and the girls flocked around. Yes I was the only teenager that had a car. Then I went to college, I was kicked out of the first and the second so my father said no more money for school. Wow do I miss the co-eds! Then there was the draft, I think my father arranged to have me drafted as he kept saying the service would be good for me. Frig, I know what is good for me, no job an allowance so I can have a good time until I can get into a school those dollars mean more than whether you go to class or not. I did get a break and 1st I went to cadet training, because of my grades, Yes I faked grades by bribing the secretary of the school. Anyway I flunked out of pilot training, I thought they would give me a nice office job, but Frig no they sent be to bombardiers school. One would have to be an idiot to flunk out of this school besides except for aiming the device on a bomb run there is no responsibilities. Yeah I write to about 10 ladies they all want the same marry me and my money and my bod, Ha-Ha."

These talks took most of our time while recuperating and I did have a chance to interview the EM, as I already knew them, you can't live with 5 other men in close proximities without knowing their life histories. I would put down the salient facts and then ask for their input.

Andy, Jim, Enos, and Ben were very young even by the standards of the AAC, Mick and I, in our early 20's, were the old men of the EM in our crew.

I took the Wayne, nose gun, Knottes, top turret Beckker, ball gun, Turner, Tail gun, together and explained our project. All were agreeable.

———

Andy Wayne's response:

"I was brought up by a strict father, a loving mother, 2 sisters, and a younger brother. Dad insisted that we go to church every Sunday. Outside of that my young years revolved around school, vacation then more school. In High School I tried out for the football team and made 3rd string. I dated many of my girl classmates but nothing romantic. After graduation I enlisted and here I am. I write home at least once a week and receive a letter from the girl next door, her name is Sue."

———

Jim Knottes' response:

"I grew up in a broken house, my father lived on the west coast, I only saw him about 3 times as I was growing and that was when he was on a business trip. Mom remarried but I kept my Fathers' name. High School was a drag I liked to read but played tennis to keep in shape. No girlfriends and write to Mom at least twice a week."

———

Chet Murray's response:

"My life has been pretty much the same as the rest of the guys'. I did play varsity basketball and won my letter. There were plenty of girls to take out to a movie or dance but no romantic involvement just good wholesome friendly classmates. I do write home as both parents objected my enlistment in the service. When I go home I plan to go to college."

———

Enos Beckker's response:

"My young life stunk. We moved month after month, Dad was a laborer and jobs were scarce, so if we got behind in the rent we moved and sometimes it was just a shack behind someone's house or out in the country, no running water and outhouses. Dad finally got on the WPA and Mom took in washing. Life was a little better so as soon as I could I enlisted. Best thing I ever did. As soon as I get out I am going to find a regular job and go to school at night if I have too. I am not going to live in poverty as my folks have. Girlfriends! Are you kidding I wouldn't even speak to a girl.

———

Ben Turner's response:

"Wow I am sure glad you are asking me about my life. Let's start at the beginning. I was born on January 1, 1924, I was an only child. Growing up I had an exciting life as Mom and Dad were professional entertainers. Dad played 3 woodwind instruments plus the drums, Mom played the piano and danced in the chorus. So my early life was out of the proverbial trunk. Along about my 9th-10th birthdays they decided to settle down. They brought a house in the suburbs and started a career in local shows. I learned to act at a very early age. In one act I would put on a Tux and stroll out on the stage and dance with them, this always brought down the crowd. Moms taught me to dance, play the piano and carry a tune. These traits helped me get along in High School and at parties I was always in demand. I became the head cheer leader in my senior year. Now let me tell you about girls or better women. Like I said I was brought up in the theater, Mom always kept me with her and that meant the dressing room, this lasted until I was 10, so women's bodies held no secrets to me. In high school when I was at a party the girls flocked around as I played the piano and I had a large repartee of songs and each one would want their favorite. I never went out with the same girl twice. Even the last one. I already told about you my last date.

Right after this session Jim came to me and confided that he was not feeling well and wanted to go see the Shrink.

"Erick I don't think I can take anymore missions. I felt like screaming after takeoff and when the attack started I could not start shooting at the enemy. Could I be endangering the rest of the guys? I have to find out." He was sobbing.

"Go ask the Major as a courtesy, then do what you think best for you." I replied.

Jim never came back to the crew. Mick became our new top turret gunner until a newly trained one could be assigned.

We were alerted the 2nd day after our rest. We had a new bomber and the Major took James, our co-pilot, Mick and I for a quick checkout ride. Strange everything was new but everything was like the old. The Major had not named this and left this job to the ground crew. When we went out to the plane that next morning there on the nose was a very barely clad picture of a young lady with 'A New Gal' written underneath. This is our newest home when flying.

CHAPTER 6

No knock on the door just the usual whisper in the ear. I knew the time 0400 and woke with a start. It was the CQ and the same message.

"You are on. So don't be late. Brief will be in the usual hut. Now answer me." He was being insistent.

"Sure I hear you, can't you forget that you didn't come around this morning or rather night. I'll go back to sleep. OK I am awake get the others up." I spoke in a whisper.

"Just your crew the others went up yesterday." He whispered back.

The routine was now etched into our memories so each one was the same and each one was different. Time seemed to stand still and in my mind's eye the guys were all the same the events all had the same bad ending. This time would be no different than the last 15 missions or so I thought.

Briefing was at the same hut and the officer in charge was the Colonel.

"Good morning men. Today we have that milk

run you have been praying for. Railroad junctions are the goal. Fighters have tried to attack and it is true they do shoot up the stock cars and some engines, they do not interrupt the time table and in hours the stock is rolling. Now we are going to try something new. Explosion of big bombs that not only put holes in the track bed but ruin the tracks by bending and ripping these steel rails. If we get a good hit on the control tower then the switching will be disrupted." The CO continued, "The bomb run is low level enabling the next in line following the leader to toggle their bombs. Major Browne will show you the maps and the recon photos. Since there will only be 2 Groups and a squad from each this will be a quick sortie and back to base by noon." The CO concluded.

This was totally unexpected. This will count as a mission and now only eight will be left. I looked around at everybody's faces, they all had smiles. Maybe the brass had gotten the message short quick missions and we go home. The parody of the song "I'll be home by Christmas," might become true.

Then the truth was coming out in the next brief by Major Browne.

"Target is the marshalling yards at the Rhine on the enemy side." The Major intoned. "You need to fly at 1500 feet so the bombs being released will not interfere with your sighting of the target. The actual area is the concentration of rails and signal towers on this outline map. It will be easy to spot as you will fly down the tracks using the river as a guide about a mile down track you will see the IP release the bombs. It's simple and the whole time from take off to landing should be 4 hours and no oxygen." The Major smiled as he ended the Briefing.

"On the photos, aren't the ACK-ACK guns in those

emplacements? It sure seems like I see a lot of guns." A voice came from the officers' side of the room.

"Of course, they are for high altitude and infantry support not for low level airplanes. Intel has gone over these and assures us that our plan is logical." The CO added.

Briefing over and some breakfast with hot coffee the mood had changed from grousing to some actual laughter. We went to preflight to takeoff and not a worry in the whole outfit.

We led the group and the with P51's escorting there were no fighters, a scout plane could be seen in the distance.

The groups' assignment was to approach the bridge then turn 90degrees to port go up the river for 15minutes make a 180 to starboard then 15 to 20 minutes to target, Navigator would make corrections to actual headings. Just before we made the first turn a B24 was sighted entering the target area.

"Holy cow what in the world is that 24 doing over our target." The pilot was almost shouting over the intercom.

"I see some bomb explosions. Now the plane is heading on our planned return. I see the tail markings it's a 'Z', so it's one of this formation." The Co pilot had the glasses and spotted the whole seen.

"This is the Pilot we will proceed to do the job we were assigned. Since the ACK-ACK is for infantry support no problem. Crew; get ready for a bumpy ride. Out:" The Major's voice was steady, no panic.

The target was in sight only our planes were at least 4 minutes from IP. The Ack-Ack started the fact was they were exploding at our altitude instead of 15000 feet. The early bird had tipped the gunners off and they had time to reload the ammo and change the fuses. As lead we got the first salvo and it rocked the ship though no one was hurt. Tail reported a ship being hit and going down with 5 chutes opening. Then starboard waist reported another hit and explosion, no chutes.

"I don't see any chutes opening and the debris is all over the sky" Reported Chet.

"G. A. the shells all over exploding near the planes." Tail was near tears while trying to remain calm.

ACK-ACK shells explode with a terrible loud bang and if close the explosion rocks the whole ship. The next shell came mighty close to the tail section.

"We are past our bomb run and the Ack-Ack is slacking," The pilot spoke just as we took a hit in the tail area. "Everybody stay at your stations RO go see what you can find. Out:"

I went through the bomb bay and saw all the bombs had been jettison. Through the waist to the tail and one look was all I needed to see that nothing could be done for Ben. The shell had literally torn the turret out of the airplane and Ben was just hanging there half in and half out of the plane. I dragged his body all the way into the waist section and covered him with a tarp. I then reported the facts back to the pilot.

"RO to Pilot, Ben has had it and the turret is useless. The structure seems ok and I noticed the stabilizers were responding to your foot commands. Over and Out:"

"Pilot to RO: Roger. Come back to your station. Out:"

When I was in the bay another explosion, only this was near and not a direct hit. I hurried to the front.

"RO that was shrapnel hitting us I think the Co Pilot took a hit see what you can do." Pilot spoke as he was struggling with the controls.

My station was right behind the Co Pilot so all I had to do was walk around the bulkhead. I heard James moaning and I looked down at the pedal controls, his leg was broken as fragments had done a lot of damage to him and the nose section. It took several minutes for Mick to come forward to help. We laid James on the seat behind the Pilot, applied a tourniquet, Mick stayed with him, until he lost conscience. Then he assumed the top turret gun position. I went to see what I could do to help the Pilot. Then I got a call from the top turret.

"I took a hit in my arm but can still function." Mick did not use the usual calling procedure.

"RO be my Co and get in his seat, then call the nose section as I believe they are in trouble. The 51's are hovering so I don't think we have any fighters to worry about." The Major was saying this as I was seating myself into the Co Pilots chair.

"RO to Nose or anyone in the nose section, answer. Out;"

"Navigator to RO, roger we have a bad situation here the nose has been hit and Andy is badly wounded, Bomb and myself are AOK. Out:"

I did not have to tell the Pilot as he was listing to the intercom.

The airplane flew very sluggish and I would help the Pilot by holding the wheel steady it was difficult to keep a heading as the tail stabilizer was responding sluggishly to the foot pedals. We were over the North Sea, the land could be seen when the clouds parted. It was raining which is not news, it will make landing very tough.

"RO I will tell you when to lower flaps, first15 degrees then full on second command, I will give you a signal to down wheels by a hand gesture, a fist on my right hand, after these duties, I will need help with landing, keep yelling the altimeter reading every 100 feet then every 50 when we reach 100 feet. As soon as tires touch ground help by applying the brakes really hard. No questions you have been checked out. With luck you and I will bring this ship to the hard stand." The Major recited this without the formal intercom answers.

"Roger." Was all I could say!

It seemed like hours and hours in reality it was just a short time before we saw the base directly ahead, I glanced at the altimeter it showed 900+ feet, this was good as we could land quickly after given the OK.

"RO, as soon as we turn into leg one, signal the ground that we have wounded aboard, use the Very gun and the yellow and white flares are to be used. The ground should signal OK using a green flare. You will have to watch for the flare." The Pilot voice was strained.

As we made a 90 degree turn, the hand signal meant wheels down I applied the lever, then it was time to signal for permission to land right away, I grabbed the Very pistol shoved it into place and fired two rounds. All this while stretching up in the seat as far as I could. The ground answered green and the Major made a 180 lined up the runway. First call was 15 degrees then on the next voice I went to full flaps. We landed but there were 2 bumps before the ship settled down and the Pilot and I applying the brakes, I was standing up in the Co Pilots seat applying the most pressure I could muster. Taxing to the hard stand ended a disastrous mission.

Everyone sighed and took a deep breath.

CHAPTER 7

THE AMBULANCE AND MEDICS HAD anticipated our arrival and were waiting. The medics came into the plane from the bomb bay, took James out and put him on a stretcher then into the waiting car. Then Andy was carried out on the shoulders of the medics. Mick climbed out on his own feet. I sat and was not thinking: I was in a stupor.

"RO thank you." The Major had leaned over and said these words I will never forget.

Everyone got out and lined up. A jeep came up to the plane and two ground execs climb into the aft section and removed Ben. The rest of us went to debrief in another truck.

Debrief room was very quiet and more crews arrived. The CO came in and no one called attention as he went to the platform.

"Men I will not deceive you, this mission was a failure. Our group lost 2 complete planes; besides those 10 men, we have two men KIA on the ships that came back. The number of wounded in the hospital stands at 6 at this moment. The other group lost 4 airplanes all downed in enemy territory. I know the question on everyones' mind, who was the Pilot on other ship that alerted the enemy, was it one of our group or the other group? I know the answer but I am not to reveal the name of the other crew they will be disciplined. Now I want this to be a very thorough briefing." This concluded the CO's debrief.

Even after the CO left the room, everyone remained very quiet; it was unusual as these were young men use to ribald jesting. The drinks were passed out and no one was refused the second libation. Even the Major who was a tee-totaler accepted a glass and I had my first drink, it burned all the way down and I thought now I know why I don't drink. Our crew or the remainder of our crew was called last.

"The shock of seeing that 24 over the target area was so great I almost called for abandonment but then it occurred at briefing the word was the shells were for high altitude, I decided to complete our mission". Our leader spoke without pointing a finger at anyone. "The shells the ground was firing were fragmentation and explosive types. This is why some planes had damage while others just blew up. I lost one man Ben Turner, Tail gunner, and three wounded Andy Wynne, Nose gunner, James Thomason Co-Pilot and Mick Raymound Engineer. I have no prognosis on them or when they will be fit for duty." Major completed his assessment and turned the report over to me.

"When hit I went to the tail section and found Ben just hanging by his parachute strap half in and half out of the ship. I pulled him into the waist and covered him, Proceeded to my station and." This is a far as I could tell what occurred I broke down sobbing. Wes and Joe came to my rescue. They literally pushed me away from the table. This ended debrief.

While we were still in the room the Ground Exec came in and went to the head table.

"We just got word from the other group. The group lost 4 planes and 12 chutes were seen to open from the four planes. Their CO reports 10 more crew members wounded no word on their condition. The crew that broke formation has been reassigned, as to its where abouts or destination this is classified information." He did not take questions.

After debrief we just stood around, perhaps waiting for orders or just a suggestion of what to do.

"Hello Mick, what are you doing here we thought you would be in the hospital chasing the nurses. How is the Purple Heart wound?" Enos asked.

"Heck the Doc's put on a powder, wrapped it up in a white bandage then said you can go back to your station. Here I am rearing to go." Mick was smiling all the time. "We must eat to keep the energy up." Mick came to the rescue. "All follow me and I will show you to the mess hall. The food will be edible and the coffee hot." Mick led the way.

"How in the hell did intelligence screw up? Why did the other 24 leave the squadron and really frig up the bad situation." I asked the question that was on every body's mind.

"Shoot that other plane was probably one of the captured planes the enemy had reconditioned and flew over by guessing our destination." A gunner from one of the other crews made the comment and the question.

"You don't suppose that they have cracked our secret codes and now know every time we hit a target." Another crew spoke up.

"No way! We change the codes every hour." I replied and was seconded by all RO's.

My mind was not concentrating on what was said and I kept wandering to the moment when I pulled Ben inside. This I told myself was nonsense, keep your mind on what was going on now. I noticed that there were other conversations going on but these seem to break off in mid thought. I was drinking coffee one cup after another. All of a sudden I felt tired and could not keep my eyes focused, it was only 1530, I got up without a word and left, others followed.

CHAPTER 8

THE NEXT DAY DAWNED AND I was up by 0630, no reveille. Mick came to just as I was leaving the hut.

"Where are you going this time of day? And in uniform, I am assuming you are off to chapel." Mick was right on.

"Want to come with me I'll wait for 5 minutes."

"I am with you give me 2 minutes for a nature call and dress OK." Mick was half dressed by the time he got the words out.

The chapel was, you guessed it a Quonset hut, we went inside and the mass had not started so approached the back and saw the priest.

"Father we lost one of our crew yesterday and I was wondering if we could have a mass said." I asked politely.

"Sergeant." The Chaplain started. "If I said a mass for everybody that was lost I would be saying Mass endlessly. I will remember you buddy especially in mass today and add him to my list that I say everyday.

Will that be alright with you? And oh will you be staying? Mass starts in 15 minutes."

"Of course we will." I added an Mick nodded without being asked.

After Mass we headed to the mess hut. Neither of us mentioned Ben or the events of yesterday. As for me I hoped that this would be the last time but I knew deep inside that I would be making this trip again, I prayed that it would not happen to me. As we approached the mess we both saw the balance of our crew waiting.

"Why are you guys waiting? Aren't you hungry after all the food can't be that bad?" Mick called out.

"Good news we have a 3 day pass to go to London if we want to go." Enos cried out to us. "I am raring to go, Piccadilly Circus, watch out."

We went inside got our trays full then sat down before the pass routine continued.

"I have been to London twice before and so count me out, besides I want to see the country side, right now it is a beautiful time to sight see." I ventured.

"Count me out too." Mick quickly added. I will go with Erick and keep him out of trouble. What about you Chet? You want to see the Circus? I know if you go with Enos you will have a good time."

"Yeah he told me about all those girls parading down the sidewalk, this I gotta see. It might be something to write home about." Enos replied.

The subject changed to speculation about a new plane or if 'The New Gal' could be repaired in time for the next flight. The word mission was not mentioned.

"They can do wonders those GI's from the repo depot.

Install a new tail turret, Plexiglas for the nose with a patch here and a patch there." Mick assured us all. "The ship will be almost new."

Without saying we knew he meant that Ben would be missed. We all walked over to the orderly hut which served as an office plus the CO's room, got our passes. Mick and I put down the closest village as it was not a town in the sense lots of houses and stores. A PUB, a Market, a Restaurant and the Meeting hall comprise the Village square. We headed to our hut stopped on the way to the mess hall picked up some 'c-rations' and whatever the cooks could spare, headed out to survey the country side. We both had bicycles, at that time of the war you either had a bicycle or walked; otherwise you stayed at the base. Going to London you caught the train which was always crowded to overflow and that meant standing the whole time which could take up to 4 hours. We tied our knapsacks to the handle bars, hopped on the bikes and started down the English back road. The roads are an experience one should take once in a lifetime. The traffic is not like in the US, the rules of the road are quite different. All vehicles are right hand drive except the US army vehicles are left hand drive so this make an interesting confrontation on the roads who has the right away. The English usually solve this by the one who uses the horn first means he goes first. The bicycle rider just takes precaution and uses good judgment that means everything that moves goes first.

Flying over the country side the striking difference from USA to here was twofold the farms are smaller and usually a hedge separates neighbor form each other, this I was told was due to the fence law enacted so a few families could not own all of Britain. Then the farms go down to the railroad within a foot or two, unlike America where the railroads own land up to the fence of the ranches. This makes bike riding very nice to enjoy the scenery.

Riding a bicycle down the back roads all the senses take over. The road we took had a canopy of trees and the branches hung over the sometimes unpaved road. The eyes could not see very far but the sights varied mile to mile. Next the smells were delightful due to the different trees and hedges, then there were the farms different crops and or animals, the barns and houses were not very far from the lane. You could hear nothing for a long stretch then an engine and horn would sound or the cows making noises heard above the quite. Feeling the sun then the shade radiating on your back was very soothing. This kept happening sending the heat and coolness on you as the road took you in and out of the trees. Then there was the great overall inner feeling of pleasure forgetting the war and just having a good time with a buddy. One time looking up we saw some airplanes just barely visible and no noise, one could not tell if they were coming home or going on a raid. It was like being home and looking up as an airliner made its regular trip.

We had ridden for about 4 hours a village should be around somewhere. There were no signs as all the signs were taken down due to the expected invasion, one had to know where one was going or you could get lost. Mick had some experience with map making and kept a log of where we were and what roads we crossed or took. It would be a help on the return.

A village came into view after a hill climb and it had a square with a few benches. The local constable was patrolling the street so we asked if we could stop and have lunch in the park.

"Yank you may use the park for lunch but you must vacate before dark, you know there is a war on? I am the Constable in this area and you can't be too careful." He was warning us "

We have a little lunch that the cook put up for our pass. Would you like to join us?" I asked.

"No thank you, I will get a cup of tea and come back. Just make yourself comfortable." He added as he walked away.

"Mick, the cook did a great job here is sandwiches and Coffee, two thermoses and 2 C-rations. This is enough for three days." Just as I spoke here came the Constable. "Will you join us? We have plenty and C-rations to boot."

"Thank you again but you must have the rations to keep your health" He spoke with authority.

"Where exactly are we? Are there any interesting places we can see?" Mick inquired.

"Now that you asked, this area is as all of Great Briton lots historical places. We have one of the oldest castle ruins in the land; there are the local Botanical gardens with a fine assortment of Roses if that's to your liking. Plenty of hiking trails but you should not venture on these without proper guide. Oh by the way my name is Constable Robert Weems, call me Mr. Weems. As you ride you may get lost just tell anyone you ask directions that Mr. Weems vouches for you. I have already checked you in the area. Your CO tells me you are members of the group. Have a nice holiday." The constable left us with a salute.

We went on our journey and by early evening we found a nice Inn. We asked for a room. At first the clerk was doubtful until we mention Mr. Weems.

"Oh you are the two young fliers he mentioned when he called. Yes we have accommodations for you a nice room with twin beds. We have prepared a supper that may be to your liking; however dinner is out of the question. Sorry showers are only allowed in the morning but you can freshen up and be ready for supper in say an hour." The clerk had this all arranged with the Constable.

It was at supper that I had a chance to interview Mick.

———

Mick Raymound"s Response:

"I was born On February 28 1917 on the farm where I have lived all my life until I enlisted. School was normal for a farm boy but by the time I was 9 raising a cow for 4H was the biggest event of my life. I did win 2nd prize, 2 years later. High School was like grade school we all knew each other. The dances were Saturday night at the local barn. Attending the square dance the height of the week, of course I went with my parents as usual in other words I can't remember not going to a Saturday night dance. I had 3 sisters, they were the big reason I am in the Army. In farming areas everyone is suppose to do his duty and the girls couldn't so the family selected me with lots of pressure from the community and the minister. Do I receive Mail? Lots from home and when I write all the families with the daughters they read my letters. When this is over I am going back home and back to farming."

We enjoyed the supper and went to bed early tired but relaxed. Next morning up early got a quick shower left a five pound note from each of us although the room rate was posted as 2 shillings ½ crown. It was worth every penny. Riding all day we found we had circled the base and now could be back by late evening. As we approached the base the CQ came out and said the CO wanted to see us. We looked askance at each other then entered the HQ Hut.

"Glad you made it back early I have two Corporals' waiting for a place to sleep. They will take the place of the Nose and Tail Gunners. Let me introduce them to you." The Ground exec called for the young fliers to come into his office. "Cpl. William Jefferes, Cpl. Harry Burnes Meet Sgts' Mick Raymound and Erick Horseman. They will show you to your new Hut and assign bunks. I wish the Best of luck to both." The exec saluted all and we left.

"Call me Erick I am the RO and this is Mick the ENG. Welcome you will meet the other two when they return from London." As we approached the Hut I led the way.

A weird feeling comes over you as the two previously occupied bunks now have the mattress rolled up and all the clothing is gone along with the contents of the foot locker. It is like no one ever used these before. "Naming the bunks one and two," Mick told Bill, already he had a nickname, "Take bunk one and Harry you will sleep in number two which happens to be the top bunk."

"You guys go get you gear and you will find a cart by the Hut and bring everything here. After you get squared away we will have a bull session and tell you what you need to know. Get going before it is too dark. Blackout regs are strict. Besides you can't see two feet in front of the cart, getting lost is not an option." Mick pointed them the way.

Bright and early revile sounded and the 4 of us went to chow that way we could learn about the new men. And I told them about the history I was writing about our crew, both thought it was a good idea and they will participate.

William Jefferes' Response:

"I was born in January 1925. School was no different than any of the other schools that millions attend in the Mid West. I was an athlete in high school and went out for all the sports but football is still my favorite, I lettered 2 years as a running back. In my school all the guys had girlfriends in the senior year my special was named Ruth. I still write her but it's not the same as when we started to send each other letters, I don't know why but the letters are different. After this is over I am going back to school, studying will be my no.1 priority"

———

Harry Burnes' Response:

"I was born on January 2nd 1925 in California right near the Ocean. School was in a very large building and we always had the max pupils in our classes. Lots of time we never really knew our classmates as they came from various areas, oh you didn't mean High School, come to think they were the same. I did some sports but my height kept me from the contact sports so I settled for Tennis. No special girlfriends, I do write to two and they answer once in a while. After this I am going back and surf and surf until I decided what I want to do in life.

About this time CQ came into the hut and said the CO wants to see all of Major's Richards crew on the double. We left pronto.

Entering the HQ hut, our squadron The Major and the rest of the crew was already milling around. The CO came out and the Exec called Attention.

"Thank you for being prompt. I have good news. Your airplane is repairable fact is one more day and the job will be completed. Next I want to introduce your new Co-Pilot Lt. Patrick O'Neall; I will not keep you long. If the plane is on line tomorrow then Major take it up for a test and check out the new Co-Pilot. One more thing your crew will be on alert day after. So enjoy the extra days off," The CO left with these words.

"I assume these two men are replacements." The Major spoke right after we left the HQ hut. "I am your Pilot and therefore Co when we are flying. On my left is Lt. Wills Navigator; on my right is Lt. Kielly Bombardier. You met Lt. O'Neall in the HQ. Have the RO and Engineer give you an orientation how we operate. It's nice to have you aboard." He ended the meeting by walking away.

MICK AND I SPENT ALL the rest of the morning getting acquainted with the new guys and then waited in the mess hut for the two others to show up from the trip to London. The train was on time. They strolled into the mess as if they didn't have a care in the world.

"Hi guys. You must be the replacements." Both said in unison.

"Boy did we have a blast in town we met a couple of nice girls. Oh how? We forgot there was an air raid and were told to go to the underground, so we went into a shelter there is where we met these ladies. We had already done the Piccadilly parade. It was just as you said nothing worth picking up. Then these girls were with their Mother and she had been to the U.S. once and recognized the uniform so we struck up a conversation. Nothing really happened, we just talked and as we left the shelter Mom invited us back the next time in London." Both were trying to speak at the same time.

Mick brought them up to date on the Plane

situation and told them about the Co-Pilot. Then dropped the bad news we were alerted day after tomorrow.

At Mess the next early morning we were told our airplane was on the line. No one had to tell or order us we as a group got our flying gear together and biked down to the line. 'The New Gal" looked great you had to inspect close up to see any damage. We did a quick pre-flight I tested the Freqs and found everything working. As I was leaving the ship up walks the Pilot and the other officers.

"Since we are all here let see if this bird still flies. RO contact tower and clear. Ok. Engr make sure we have adequate fuel and you gunners we will fly to the wash and you can test your marksmanship. Everybody prepare to board." The Major had spoken.

So we hoped to it and in 15 minutes we were on the tarmac ready for takeoff. It was a beautiful day to fly and the ship was certainly air worthy. I set the Radio compass for the wash. This is really a half bay and target ships are in line for bomb and machine gun practice. I kept the radio on so everyone could hear then looked around the corner and sure enough the Co-Pilot was at the controls. He was a smooth flyer and I thought I hope we never have to fly home with him as our leader, we are satisfied with the Major; this was selfish I just did not want anything more to happen.

That evening there was something new posted on the bulletin board a notice of the crews that were alerted an ours was listed. Again we were the only crew in our hut, the reason was simple there were 3 squadrons' each assigned to a different squad. The reason is obvious.

"Alright you lucky guys up drop em and grab your socks it is time to get up." CQ was having his fun as the other

12 had been given a pass and we were the only ones in the hut.

"CQ, you are the only one I know that can make waking up at 0400 and make it sound as if you are staying at the Waldorf. Get lost we are up." I almost yelled at him.

The rest of the routine is almost the same latrine, dress and leave for the Briefing. Only in a daze I called one of the new men 'Ben", the others looked at me.

"I am sorry, it just slipped out. I'll be more careful." I felt like I wanted to kick myself for the mistake..

Brief had a surprise as the Target was the Pens and possibility of weather so the alternate was the wharves. This is always a 50-50 chance between hard missions with fighters dogging our every move followed by ACK-ACK, and a nice easy one with moderate flack.

Preflight was routine as we had given the ship a run yesterday and the Pilot was satisfied of course we half redlined the log this was precaution if we happened to crash on takeoff.

Takeoff was at 0700 as the other squadron lead our flight, we would be top starboard the ground gunners would have plenty of time to adjust to our headings and altitude. In other words we would be the sitting ducks.

Luck was on our side I was monitoring the call back freq when the order came to change course.

"RO to Pilot, change channels to #4 a very important message. Over out:" I contacted the flight deck and all who were listing.

"Pilot to Navigator, we have a change of target, set your course to the Warf area. Out:" He did not need to tell all as everyone was listing after I had called the Pilot.

This turned out to be the milk run everyone had been hoping for.

We dropped our bombs, no fighters and very little flack, then we headed home, we would be in time for a late lunch at mess. 'Hurray', this was number seventeen really eighteen but the brass decided that the one we had been recalled after 6 hours didn't count. The life as a bomb crew when counting is life itself.

The next two missions were washed out. This is the time we got to know each and the dreams and hopes of the individual shared with your buddies. I told of my hope when this war was over that I could go back to college finish my degree and possible teach with writing as a pastime.

"Come on Erick; tell us about the girls just waiting for you so 'the one' can marry you and raise a dozen kids." Laughingly joke Enos.

"Yes I do write two young ladies but they are classmates while I was in high school, friends of the family and next door neighbors. I wouldn't marry either one although I like them as friends. I had one girl in college but as soon as I left she married a ROTC major when he was commissioned. I may meet someone who makes my heart flutter as the saying goes though I am a practical person and would want someone who has the same goals that I have." I ended the speech as I was losing my audience.

"I want to go home and raise crops and cattle. I sure hope that little girl that used to be my partner at the square dances is still single; I might try and court her." Mick entered the session.

'Oh don't tell me the strong silent guy with the bull as long as the day has a glint in his eye for the ladies. This is so different from the buddy we all know." Enos again was teasing.

"Enos teasing! Why the whole time we went to London you teased me about everything I hold dear, nothing was sacred." Chet countered.

This went on for some time with each taking his shot and being the butt of the next joke. This is how you build friendship in the war it lets you forget what is next.

Next day the next big disappointment was on the bulletin board. The notice was over the signature of the General, Commanding 8th AAC. 'Notice to all flying personnel. This order shall take effect immediately. The new goal will be 30 Missions. Missions will be approved by 1st Squadron Commander, 2nd Group Commander, and 3rd AAC Commander. The exceptions will be for those who have completed 23 Missions. Or if by enemy fire the airplane was downed then 25 missions will be the goal of those crews. Signed XXX, Commanding.

The order really hit home. Our only out would be if they counted when we bailed and the ship crashed into the North Sea. Our CO said he would check it out and let us know.

Then in succession was 2 missions both with plenty of ME 109's and FW190's, By now the AAC has devised wing gas tanks for our P51' and P47' enabling these to escort us to just about any target that was given us. B24's could carry more tonnage and fly longer than the more famous B17. The enemies capital was dedicated to the 17 groups. This did not make us unhappy. From all basis in Briton the flight was 14 hours and meant that wing gas tanks had to be full, This makes all bombers a flying gas station and subject to an early explosion. Although the ground crew said it was just a matter of time when our ships will have these tanks installed.

CHAPTER 10

THE NEXT TWO MISSIONS WERE long we revisited the factory but with escort so all we had to contend was the flack. Our Pilot was adept at dodging the bursts. The consensus among the fliers was that the enemy was short on ammo. At least it was wishful thinking. Then we tried the Marshalling yards this time from 25000 feet no one broke formation. Camera planes had taken photos of the yards and the damage was considerable. This time every bomber would carry the very large explosive with delayed time fuses. Maybe we wouldn't have to return again.

It happened to me on our return to base. I was at the port waist gun, a Me109 came from 12O'clock low and by the time he was in my sphere enabling me to shoot he was even. Aiming right at the gun port, his bullets were striking the fuselage. I froze, I panicked, until I saw the flashes of gunfire from his machine guns then I lost everything I was taught in gunnery school. Short bursts one or two seconds then re-aim and shoot again. I held the trigger until I saw my rounds hitting the canopy. He made a rolling dive carrying him to the front then rolled over and was going straight down I did not see a chute open. I was sick; I thought I had killed a human being. Instead of relief or jubilation, I was devastated. Right then the Ball gunner reported the Pilot had bailed and a chute was opening. I was frightened, I had wet my pants. I could not relate this to the rest of the crew. So later I fabricated a story that I had spilled my coffee. No one ever questioned me. This episode taught me a lesson. One can function even when he believes he is facing certain death. The fact never the less does not remove the taste in your throat or the abject fear you have that this may be your last anything.

Damage to our 'The New Gal' was minor and only the tail gunner Harry received a wound. He received the Purple Heart award but didn't lose any time. The Medics bandage him up and marked him fit for duty, not even an aspirin.

We now had twenty two Missions but were in limbo, no word as from the top if they would count our being shot down as the Brass put it 'action due to enemy fire'.

There is an old army saying 'hurry up and wait'. I believe that flying on raids spoke volumes that prove the old ways were wise. After a mission everyone could hardly wait for the next to happen as that meant closer to going home, as the time neared for this event to occur the time seemed to stand still leaving one wondering, how long before they,(the Brass) will make up their collective mind.

Time and time again we were posted on the board only to be rained out. This at least let the ground crews to repair and replace the planes. At last the weather looked good and the posting showed that we were scheduled.

Word got around the huts that this would be a very large

contingent of bombers and that it would be an important target some speculation was it was the anticipated 2nd front. Surprising how fast these rumors spread. The first time was in the mess hut and returning to the bunk some swore it was true they had heard his from reliable sources. We would find out the truth the next briefing.

"Ok everyone up and no lagging as briefing is due at 0500. All EM go to the mess tent and woe to the one who is late. The Colonel is giving both sides of why and where, you got it, now up and at them." CQ was in loud voice as all would be up. The part about a large contingent was true.

All the EM from all squadrons accounted for and not only coffee but real toast, milk and oleo were provided. This was going to be big.

"Attention!" given by the Sgt Major as the CO came in under the blackout curtains.

"Men at ease you may finish the snack provided but no smoking." The Col in his usual tone spoke. "We are going to bomb the mainstay of the enemy. Ball bearings! That's right no machinery can move without these little pieces of metal." He held up a small ball bearing. "Now this will be a very large numbers of planes it is essential that everything is coordinated. So every job on every airplane is important. You will have escort by the P51's and P47 and a newcomer P38. You will encounter heavy flack but the fighters will or should I say be kept under control by our guys. This bombing has taken place once before and intelligence declared that 90% of the factory was hit; now we want the factor to be 100% destroyed. I know that will do your utmost to make this a successful mission.

"Attention!" The order as given by the Sgt as the CO left.

Some murmuring among the tables but it mostly subdued. Then the Major came in to complete the brief.

"A new radio device had been installed on all lead planes it was called IFF short for Identification Friend or Foe. This would be the responsibility of the ROs to destroy, if landing in enemy territory, 'A' red button in the radio compartment when pressed detonates a small charge in the box. This will happen only when the wheels are down on the ground in enemy terrain. The signal will be encoded and if Ok will be nothing if enemy a loud shrill note will sound on selected Freqs. The Major continued briefing, all technical terms. He then left the Hut.

What followed was the usual routine. Our Pilot added keep the eyes open.

Take off was on schedule and all headed for assembly point. As we approached it was hard to believe the amount of planes circling as we were lead we took up our position. The Co-Pilot fired a flare and we were off wave after wave probably 500 to 600 planes in formation.

As soon as we crossed the channel here came in sight their fighters only to me met by our defenders. Dog fights after dogfights took place too many to keep track and no way knowing which airplane shot down the other. As we got close to the factory area the ACK-ACK started and the enemy planes left. Our escort went out of range and waited for our return. The flack was something fierce with so many to shoot at it meant no one was being picked on. As lead we had a lot to fly through but as soon as we got over target the guns wet silent. We dropped our ton mostly incendiaries and as usual Joe hit the Aiming Point right on the button.

"Dang I got a piece of shrapnel right in the leg. Can

someone bring be a bandage." Harry our new tail gun forgot to use the proper intercom procedure, who could blame him his first mission and he is the recipient of a purple heart.

Mick went aft and took care of Harry. About 10 minutes later he came in deck and gave me then the Pilot thumbs up, meaning the wound was not serious.

"Shoot if I could get wounded then that's the kind I would want. A small wound that would bled a lot but just scraped by the leg. The metal got stuck in Harry's chair so he will have a souvenir, and a purple heart." Mick reported to me in my ear.

The rest went as we expected the fighters returned and our escort came right after them. Bill told us then at debrief that he saw 2 Me109s'go down in flames with a P47 on their tail. As soon as we landed and taxied to the hard stand Bill went to the aid station. Rest of us went to debrief, we had some shocking news, 2 of the crews of our group reported down, Major Browne also said the 31 total planes had been lost on this raid that would mean 5% of the attacking force was lost. What this doesn't show is that meant 310 men had lost their lives on one mission, and this was considered a successful raid. We left debrief more somber than when we entered.

This ended our 23rd mission, only Bill was wounded. He was back to duty that very day.

Lord Haw-Haw was on the wireless that evening telling us how bad our aim, that we missed the target by about a mile. He ended saying Major Richards should have more practice on the bombing runs. He then listed 10 of the crews that were shot down saying that they were being taken care. The gathering of GI's around the radio, comments from our side were very crude.

Number 24, starting a countdown early this time around,

were more of the same, factories and railroad marshalling yards. More ACK-ACK each time but their accuracies were much off the mark and the ME's just made one or two passes, then chased off by the 51's. Fewer losses by our group, maybe we will make it after all. Never, never make dreams too often you might be disappointed.

Number 25, if only if the Brass would let us know the decision on that one, then we could really relax as this would be the next to last, losing one engine to flack didn't stop this plane making home. Amazing how much damage a B24 can take and still fly. One of the ground crew counted the patches on the fuselage and added up to 165. A wonder all haven't been wounded.

Finally a rain out and passes all around but not to London just local things. Mick and I decided to return to the Inn and called ahead for reservations, we added Enos just to keep things light. The Inn Keeper said they were delighted and one more would be welcome in fact it would be nice to add another. We decided on Chet and rang the Keeper adding Chet.

Four of us saddled up the bikes and once again the cooks furnished us with knapsacks full of goodies. Stopping along the way to see Mr. Weems, this time he did have coffee with us. He wondered if we had heard about the Buzz bombs that the enemy was launching towards London, we were non committal.

"Those gunners do not know the direction to London. One hit here about a mile and a half to the west. It landed in a field tore up some fallow ground and blew down a tree that was over hundred years old. Blimey if they want to waste bombs that way the war will be over sooner." Constable Weems wanted to talk and we listened. "I suppose that you lads will be going home soon. I will miss you Yank fliers, not the usual kind of soldiers that just want to brag about the U.S. and how many rooms the Master has and Oh My the number of girls kissed. Makes one to think may we should have kept the colonies, eh what." He added with a wink.

We peddled the rest of the way not stopping for a break; we got there for 'tea'. I had envisioned tea just that with mainly ladies sitting around sipping from cups. Was I ever mistaken? Tea meant the afternoon snack with biscuits and or sweets and in better times some kind of spread. This is how we were treated at the Inn. Afternoon was walking or napping just doing what pleased you. Supper, a delightful repast of cold cuts and bread pudding along with tea, the inn keepers tales of the local history kept our interest. We enjoyed the evening with conversation and music. When the evening news came on the BBC a lady, the only employee of the Inn, tuned off the radio.

"I thought everybody listened to the BBC especially the news?" I asked our hosts.

"Only when we don't have guests, the news is so freighting and most come to our area just to get away from the war and the news." Lady hostess replied. "Besides you gentlemen know firsthand what is going on and the outcome of your bombing. So why bother with these horrid stories, besides we rather hear about you and you home in the States." She added with a very nice smile.

"You can't argue with logic like that. I like getting away from the crowded military life; I was raised on a farm where our nearest neighbor was a ½ mile away." Mick joined in.

Arising early without someone rousing for a mission was a novelty. We had a nice breakfast said our goodbyes and rode our bikes back to the base and reality.

CHAPTER 11

It was late afternoon when we arrived at the base we were joking that we would be in time for mess, then we noticed the crowd around the bulletin board. We rode right up to the edge of the crowd all were saying this must be a big run. When we elbowed ourselves in position Chet read aloud the following memo. Attention all flying personnel: There will be a briefing at 0230 hours: Uniform of the day will be class 'A': All flight gear will be ready for pick up by 0230. You must be on time: Signed Gen. Commanding.

"We better park our bikes, get to the hut and get everything ready then go to mess. Maybe someone will have the scoop on where we are going. All I know is if briefing is at 0230 then it is going to be one long flight." Enos was right on.

"Since it mentions everybody it will be a big formation maybe all the aircraft in Britian. I would assume that we are going to hit something vital maybe the capital, wouldn't that be something to tell everybody back home." I was talking to all our guys.

"I am ready to chow down. The tea and crackers were good but I need good old army food," Mick, who was always ready for food, chimed in.

When we finally got to mess there sat the other two members of our crew.

"Did you hear? HQ has given the OK on our mission so now we will be on the 26th, so that means Mick and Erick will be going home after this and we that are left will have a new Pilot, Bombardier, and Navigator. Aren't you guys sad that you can't stay around? HA-HA:" laughed Harry.

"Are you guys joking? Who told you this? Don't kid around this is serious. I just want this whole war to over and we all can do what we really like to do in this world." I was frowning while I said this.

"No kidding. The Major came by and told us then he said be sure that we repeated this to you. For the Major he seemed very happy about the news. I don't think he would kid anybody about this." Harry was serious.

The whole mess was quiet this evening. No one had heard any rumors just a lot of guessing, from transferring the whole group over to the mainland to bombing every city in enemy territory and even as I had said the Capital. Consensus was it would be a long trip there and back.

Back at the hut we were getting everything ready when a member one of the other crew had written a letter and wanted one of us to hold to be mail if anything happened to him. He could not find any takers.

"Just put it in your footlocker with a note attached to be mailed in case of my demise and sign the note. The ground Exec will probably be the one to go through your effects and will have to write to your next of Kin if anything happens." I spoke with some knowledge from what happened when Ben was KIA.

"This isn't to my family; they don't know that I got a girl in a family way before I left. I have the insurance with her name on it but! Oh I don't know what to do. I am confused and not thinking right." He was almost crying.

"Hey, I know what you should do go right over to the Chaplin tell him the story and ask him if he can mail the letter. I am afraid he must read it if he needs' to send it. This would be to censor purposes." This came from one member of his crew

He hurried and went directly to the chapel-hut. After about an hour he came back to our hut and he was smiling.

"The chaplain said he would take care of this and if it needed to be mailed he would see that it would be done quietly. He even asked if he could get in touch with the young Lady maybe offer some help or advice in particular what were the government responsibilities. He said he would not divulge any of this to my family unless the person wants the parents to know." He sounded relieved.

Next morning very early the CQ came in to the Hut.

"Come on everybody up and get moving its 0145, and this briefing is very important. Not only the Colonel but the General is here so as the army says this is the big one. Now everybody in unison say 'get lost'." CQ was trying to be cheerful.

You expect this day will arrive and wonder what kind of reaction you will feel. Mostly relief the waiting is over this one last mission and then home. What if something bad happens? Like being shot down then imprison in a POW camp for the duration. Or worse shot down wounded and …. Whoa let's not have bad thoughts let's be positive nothing is going to happen except we bomb a target. All these thoughts kept running through my head. All of a sudden it was time to go to brief. We left our flight gear outside the hut with our plane number in plain sight.

The mess hall was full and the noise deafening until the Sgt Major called attention. Then you could hear a pin drop, only thing we could hear was Major Browne marching to the front of the mess.

"At ease men: This is our assignment today the capital of the enemy. Your airplane commander will have the details. With so much at stake listen to what I have to say, this will be the first 1,000 plane raid, you heard it right 1,000 airplanes in formation. Our CO will lead and Major Richards will be the right wing. The first two echelons will continue to the east and land in our ally's airport take on fuel and ammunition, the next day return home. You will have escort to the coast and those going further the Ally will escort all the way to his airfield and back to the coast. Why this target? Because this is the heart of the enemy and where his communications are centralized the target is vital for an end to this conflict. I will not take any questions. However the Priest, the Minister and the Rabbi asked for 15 minutes. After that a quick breakfast then to your ships. All the ground personnel have asked me to wish everyone good luck and return home safely." Exec's voice was filled with emotion.

I can't remember eating. I did drink a lot of coffee and immediately had an upset stomach. Since we would be the first taking off right after the CO, we better be quick and thorough with preflight. The Major was waiting beneath the Starboard wing just as he always has in past missions. We gather around.

"Men I do have a few words I want to say. As you realize I am no speaker but I want you all to know I appreciate the efforts that everyone has done to make our crew the best. Now for all to know this is my last mission as well l as Lt. Wills and Lt. Kielly, not to forget this applies to Sgt Raymound, and Sgt Horseman. The rest will receive their next assignments when we return. I am sure everybody knows I was raised in a strict religious envoirment and I never use profanity, it is frown upon, I will continue this until I leave as airplane commander. Thank you and now let's get to work." The Major had spoken in heartfelt manner.

Take off was orderly. With that many planes waiting you would think that confusion would reign. As we taxied up to the start line the 1st plane was half down the runway, as soon as his wheels were off the ground the flare was given for us to start our run. Then in turn the others followed until all 21 were in the air.

At assembly point it looked like all the airplanes in the world had assembled over England. Commanding General took the lead then our Major followed into the wing position. One 360 turn and all our squadron was on the way.

"Pilot to all: It will probably be at least an hour our escort comes into view then within the next hour we can expect the enemy. Don't tighten up but keep watch and guns keep the turrets turning. Erick and Pat will bring around the coffee and a surprise, doughnuts made especially for this flight. Over and out:" The major sounded reassuring.

"Tail to Pilot: You can't see behind us but the whole sky is filling up. Out:"

"Pilot to all: Our escorts are at 11 o'clock high and coming fast. No shooting and no testing of the guns. Out:"

Time seems to go so quickly when going into a combat zone. The first report came from the Bill the nose gunner. Then the action started.

"Nose, a FW at 11 o'clock low, in a slow roll."

"Top, 2 more diving at 3 o'clock watch out both being chased by." Mick never finished as he was firing the .50 caliber.

"Tail, I got one."

"Pilot to all, do not yell, be calm and we will understand better than screams."

"Tail, one plane in squadron 3 is going down. It is spinning."

All of a sudden the enemy fighter pulled away and the ACK-ACK started but only one battery and last less than 2 minutes.

"Pilot to all, just a single gun, there will be more shells later. Right now the enemy is trying to figure out where we are heading, they are seeing more planes than we can as their radar is picking up the whole formation.

When we reached the outer limits of target area the ACK-ACK picked up again. Shells were exploding all around us, most intense antiaircraft fire ever encountered. As we were leading the gunners were picking on larger targets which meant the airships behind us were getting the worst of the barrage.

"Tail, since last reported I have seen two more go up in flames.

"Waist to Pilot: Just saw a B17 loose a wing she spun, inside spin but 3 chutes opened.

"Tail to Pilot: Another ship just went down in a dive couldn't tell what kind as it was way back.

"Ball to Pilot: that last blast was about 500 yards below us.

"Pilot to Crew: we are coming up to IP so no more reporting. Let's let the Bombardier do what he came this far to do."

It seem like it took all day before we hear the words 'Bombs away' but as soon as he uttered the slogan Major gave it full power and we left for the allied landing strip. Only the first wave would continue east this was to clear the bomb run for the rest. It was a two hour run. I think we caught the enemy by surprise as no fighters followed the formation. Occasionally we could see ACK-ACK but only a few guns and the bursts were off to one side. We landed without any additional damage.

Greetings by our allies were exuberant, bottles of vodka sprang up like magic, Major did not imbibe neither did I. Restraint by the rest was hearting as we must load and leave by early AM. Carts of ammo came with the food and the gasoline trucks had plenty of Hi Octane, Eric watch the filling of the fuel, Enos made sure all the guns had enough of the .50 caliber to last the next day. Something hot was put into the thermos but it did not taste like American coffee.

Major Richards had embarked as soon as we landed and was in consultation with a counterpart and most of the 24's commanders. After an hour or so he headed our way. We met under the starboard wing.

"Good news and Bad news. The gasoline had been brought in by tankers for this very reason. Ammunition likewise and it is fairly fresh, we should not have jammed guns. The food is the best they can serve and I have tasted some and it is good tasting, what is being served as coffee is the drink that their soldiers use all the time, it is not alcoholic. Now the bad news the enemy has shot down 8 of our first echelon. We will be staying with the ship all night. Our friends will bring blankets and a few mattresses and can be used as a bed on the tarmac. First call will be at 0430 and take off at 0530. Our allies will escort us as far as the north coast then in about 1to2 hours we will have our own escort. The route will take us away from the large cities, but you can be assured there will be enemy fighters. Get some sleep and rest." Our Major gave a long talk, but very informative.

What he did not say was each one would have to pull guard duty, Patrick made the assignments. He figured about 9 hours, on the ground with preflight and takeoff included with 10 that would make uneven amount for each it was settled that the Major would not have guard duty. Assignments were taken without regard to rank; I pulled the 4th hour about midnight. The EM slept on the center of the waist as the Officers took up the flight deck. At 0430 we awaken by a loud bugle call from our allies.

Takeoff was without problems as their ground crew had been involved with landings and takeoffs.

Around 0900 the Mig's left us and the enemy must have been waiting for here they came, guns blazing.

"Top turret; I see 4 Fw's at 3O'clock. Out:"

"Pilot to crew: Report your gun then what you see. Don't step on another's report. Out:"

"Tail; the 109's are waiting outside not attacking. Out"

"Nose. 190's at 1"Oclock high. Out"

"Nose. Fw's at 2"Oclock and coming in. Out."

Just at that moment noise of machine gun fire could be heard all over the ship. Zing was the sound I heard as a bullet seared into my butt. I did not have the intercom on so when I said ouch no one heard. I really was in pain but I knew I could bear it out. I was frighten, TS as the guys would say. But I stayed my position. Grabbed a first aid kit and a compress put it on the wound and kept right on listening.

"Navigator to Pilot. Bombardier has been hit and from the looks of the bullet entry I am afraid it is serious, in fact I am sure he has died. Out."

"Pilot to crew. Keep calm this won't last too much longer; I can see our escorts in the distance. They are early. Out"

And they were early by at least 1 hour, but we won't remind them of this just thank heavens.

After the P51's came to our rescue we settled down and waited for instructions.

"Pilot to crew. I want everyone to report damage. Let's start with Navigator and then Nose followed by RO, Top, Port waist, Star waist, Last Tail. Include wounds. Out."

"Navigator to Pilot. I don't see much damage just a few holes from the bullets both coming in and going out. The Bombardier caught it in the forehead. Nothing we can do I have covered him with some blankets that were left from last night. Out."

"Nose to Pilot. No damage I can see our leader ship, it looks like they caught some damage to the front and the nose wheel in hanging down. Out."

"RO to Pilot. I took one in the rear, it is stopped bleeding. The radio equipment is working ok. Out."

"Engineer to Pilot. So far everything is AOK but I am still checking. Oh the fuel tanks are intact, no leaks." Out."

I can't remember what actually had transpired between the time I was wounded, and the landing and taxi. I was in pain, didn't want anyone to know how bad I was hurting, I just carried on as if nothing happened. After shutting down the engines and the medics boarded I was carried off and went in what was called an ambulance, to the base hospital. Shock set in when I was told that Joe Kielly was dead; undoubtedly the same fighter that wounded me was one of fighter's bullets that got Joe.

NEXT DAY MAJOR RICHARDS CAME to visit and to bring news.

> "Sgt. Horseman, how are you doing? I understand from the Doctors that the wound is not life threaten but is serious. You will be taken back to the states and then the decision will be yours." He called me by rank and name instead of RO, I reasoned we were no longer on flying status. He continued. "I have been asked to stay and become part of HQ staff, if I accept I will be a LT. Colonel. You will receive the Purple Heart, The air Medal, and I have put you in for the Silver Star for the performance not only in this raid but for the leadership on previous missions. Sgt. Raymound is scheduled for rotation to the USA. We lost Lt. Kielly as you know I am recommending that he too receive the Silver Star for outstanding marksmanship on many bombing Missions.

CHAPTER 12

That leaves Lt. Wills to decide to stay and become a Captain and train new Navigators or be reassigned to HQ," He concluded with a salute and left.

"Hey buddy, you think I would leave you without coming by, boy were you wrong. The other guys have been reassigned; actually they will remain with 'The New Gal', and guess, the name of the new pilot. Right Lt. Now Captain O'Neall, Harry and Bill along with Enos have gone to London. Now let's talk about you?" Mick looked great and was in high spirits. "Have you been chasing the nurses? When are you going home? I'm scheduled to leave next train out of here and catch a ship out of Scotland. Hope it's a fast one?"

"Mick! Are you going to let me say a word or two, or am I going have to yell. I may not be here very much longer they are putting me on a hospital ship back to the states any day. What I want is your address, when I write the history of our crew I might want to mail you a copy, maybe!" I told him rather than ask.

"There I go again running off and not listing. Of course I want a copy but better still why don't you come and visit. We could see my farm. Did I tell you My Dad brought the acreage down the road about a mile and put the deed in my name! Crazy huh, I'm on my own when I get home, maybe I will look up that ole girl I courted before I left. Oh I did not tell you that, yes I really did court her, told her I would marry if she waited? Now I will have to get married I have a farm and a little old house. Then what will I do?" Mick was blushing as he told me about his plans to marry.

After swapping stories about our time together at this base Mick gave me a big smile and left. Two days later I heard he left. I wasn't far behind as the medic's took me to a train for Edinburgh. A hospital ship was waiting and I was on board for the trip home.

Home, isn't that what we have hoped and prayed these months? Now that it was actually happening I couldn't envision what 'Home' meant. Was as it the enlistment ads indicated, a wife, family, or Mom and apple pie. When I thought about the meaning I thought about the evenings at the old homestead, quite, reading with the radio playing or a record on the phonograph. Sometimes I would think about the idle days of high school, these turned into very busy times with studies at college. I never dreamed about bombs falling on American Cities or in any way an invasion on U.S. Soil. I am sure that if you asked 1000 GI's the question "what does home mean to you?', you would get 1000 different answers.

So as I was lying on my stomach I took the time to try and answer that question plus others. My first thoughts were what I am going to do if they discharge me? Probably go back to college, this scares me what happens if I can't study or that the classes I have already taken are no longer in use or the credits are no longer transferrable? Then something happened that I would have never believed. On ship board the army had provided a shrink to help the returning veteran with these very questions. It took me only two sessions to figure out that returning to college was the best course of action. I made a pledge to myself right then college and a degree, then and only then would I venture into the dating scene or thoughts of the opposite sex.

"Surprise, it's me, James Thomason your old Co-Pilot. I heard that you were on board, found you on the ships record and here I am, minus one leg. I am sorry I should not have tried to put humor into our first meeting."

"Oh I don't mind it sure breaks the monotony of this voyage. It is great seeing you again."

"I wanted to see you back at the base but the Doc's forbid any visitors except the Major. I really wanted to thank you for what you did for me on that fateful flight. The Major said that it was you discovered that I had been hit and with the help of Mick you pulled me out of my seat, put on a tourniquet and then watched over me until we landed. I think it was you and Mick that saved my life. Thanks a million."

"You would have done the same for me." What next? Are you going to be discharged?"

"I don't know. Can I call you Erick and please call me James we are no longer officer to EM that's gone, water that has already gone over the dam. You know that I can no longer play baseball, and that is depressing. I suppose I will go back to college, but no scholarship, the university would not want a broken down jock taking up space."

"Hey don't start feeling sorry for yourself. I have an idea why don't you go see the Head Doctor, he did wonders for me. For your further consideration why don't we try and go to school together. You will have the GI Bill and so will I. Just mull it over and we still have 3or4 days on this ship. Oh where are they sending?"

"I am going to Colorado, the AAC has a rehab hospital for amputees they say I will be there for 6 months then free from the Army."

"Say that is exactly the place the Doc is sending Me. Oh you didn't know I am the original 'half-ass' veteran I got a bullet in the place you sit down. No reconstructive surgery but they do have pads and pillows to make life easier."

"OK but let's keep in touch we can have mess, there I go

good old army jargon, any way there is no rank on the ship we can have lunch in the dining room together. I am in the 2nd group what about you?"

I have been taking lunch here in the ward but today they release me and I can walk so I will put in for 2nd seating. OK see you tomorrow. 'James!"

We had lunch the next day and traded stories about the whole crew, no back biting just good memories. James said he had an appointment with the shrink that afternoon and would see me the next day for lunch.

As it turned out we had lunch every day and then after we reached the rehab we had lunch and dinner just about every day. That's when we discovered a lot in common about our desire to teach, and to not just teach but help kids and their families understand about life and that war is not the answer. One lunch about 4 months into this rehab James had an Idea.

"The war is over for us and it looks like it will be over in Europe in the short term. I contacted my school about the scholarship and as was expected no longer valid but they are accepting students with the GI Bill eligibility. I put in my name and was immediately accepted. I put in your name and was told you had the best chance since you knew me so here is a name and a number call, register for the fall semester."

While we had a respite from the hospital routine and before classes started James and I had a real heart to heart talk. He was fearful that a one legged man would be looked upon as handicapped and that going back for a degree in business was a waste of talent and time. He had so wanted a career in sports and he thought this was impossible.

"Look, James, some of the sports figures that have become

heroes to many youngsters had a handicap. Why don't you continue with your major and supplement with a course that many of the high schools need, like government or history, then you will have two skills to offer any prospective employer. I know there are plenty of schools that need a coach though budget restraints limit the amount they can pay for a coach only. Why not give it a try. If plans don't work out you have the disability money to try something else. I will promise I won't get up and walk away. OK."

"Erick you have a way with words. I will give it a go."

TIME HAS SLOWED DOWN COMPARED to the time overseas. James and I graduated and he got a job as a teacher and coach in a town near where we went to College. I found a job teaching classes at an intermediate school in the same area. James met a very nice teacher and they were married. I am afraid that the marriage bug just never got to me. Oh I dated many young ladies but the relationships turned out to be platonic. I keep writing and the rejection slips kept coming.

One day James called me and said let's meet for dinner at one of our favorite restaurants. I asked if his wife Jenny was invited he said oh yes.

"Hi Erick, sit down we haven't ordered. I have a beer how about coffee for you?"

"Sounds good, Hi Jenny, keeping this guy in line," I looked at James as I said this.

"Erick, I heard from Colonel Richards today. Seem he traced me through the old pilots association. Anyway he wanted to know if I knew where you were living I told him about us and he wanted me to deliver a message.

OK." He paused to see my reaction.

"I never expected to hear from the Col. He was always so uptight about having a conversation with Enlisted Men. I suppose that that has changed since the war is over. What did he want with me?"

"You remember Joe Kielly, of course you do. Seems his father contacted the Col and has arranged to have Joe exhumed and brought back to his home town and is to be buried with the whole army regimen. I guess this has cost Mr. Kielly a lot of money. He has offered to pay your way to Washington to pick up the casket then bring it back home. He will pay all our way to and from. I am to go with you. The Col has contacted Wes and Mick and they will be there for the reburial. Naturally I could not answer for you but here is his number if you want to call him. I hope you will say yes. It will take all of our spring vacation. I told him I may want to bring my wife and he ok's that. But Jenny wants to stay home with the baby."

"I will call him as soon as I get home. I want to go and I will have the history printed so he can have a copy. Let's make the reservations and he can reimburse us or whatever makes him happy, you know that he and his father did not get along, maybe this will bring closure."

All the old crew met at Mr. Kielly's home and graciously had a dinner for all which included the Col. Each had a chance to talk to the others before Enos, Mick and I went outside and exchanged what had happened since the last time we were together. Nothing spectacular, Mick had married the girl he had proposed way back when and now they were expecting their third child. Enos had gone back to school majored in electronics and now was employed in a very lucrative position. I gave everybody a copy of the book 'A New Gal'. For Mr. Kielly I gave him Joe's copy then when I got the chance I told him what Joe had said about their relationship and that he was going back to school so he could join his Father in business.

"Joe wrote me and told me about the book. In the letter he said he would like you to get together with me. He went on to hint that there might be a surprise for me. I now know what he meant. T.G.

Interment in the family plot took place the next day.

When I was in the teens some of my Fathers friends that had served in WWI passed away and they had a Military Honor Guard. The Burglar sounded Taps, the other three of the guard had rifles and each fired 3 rounds. Each time I attended this ceremony I cried, I cannot explain why. I knew each of the deceased as they came to see Dad on special occasions. I also knew some of their sons either at school or camp. As there were no close relationships, I would wonder why I cried.

Attendance was large and expected the director had chairs for everyone and Mr. Kielly had arranged for the Colonel to sit next to him followed by the rest of us. The Colonel gave a short eulogy ending reading the citation with the Silver Star then the Purple Heart. I was asked to say a short prayer. Then Taps followed by the Three Gun Salute, I openly sobbed.

As we left each one promised that he would keep in touch with the rest. This never happened.

THE END